When Frank Was Four

Alison Lester

Houghton Mifflin Company

 # One

When Nicky was one she spilled spaghetti on her head.

Frank bit the dog.

Tessa took her first steps.

Celeste ate the cat food.

Ernie banged the
pots and pans.

And Rosie said 'Horse'.

But Clive smashed the china
at his Great Grandmother's birthday party.

Two

When Frank was two
he loved to wave
goodnight to the moon.

A kangaroo stole
Rosie's french fries.

Tessa stopped wearing
diapers.

Ernie climbed into the fish tank.

Celeste began to sleep all night.

And once at the supermarket, Clive just couldn't wait.

But Nicky got lost on Christmas Eve.

Three

When Clive was three he danced in his cousin's tutu.

Ernie gave away his pacifier.

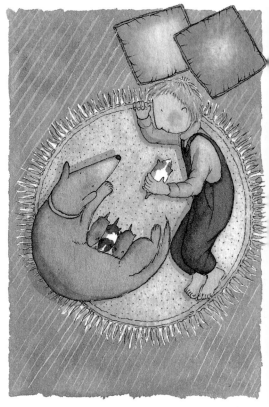

Frank's dog had puppies.

Rosie began to play
the guitar.

Celeste was given a
chicken for her
birthday.

And Nicky got stuck
up a tree.

But Tessa made a cake.

Four

When Frank was four he ate three bags of candy fish.

Nicky cut off her braid.

Tessa dressed up the cat.

Ernie started to wear glasses.

Clive took off his training wheels.

And Rosie's pony arrived on Christmas morning.

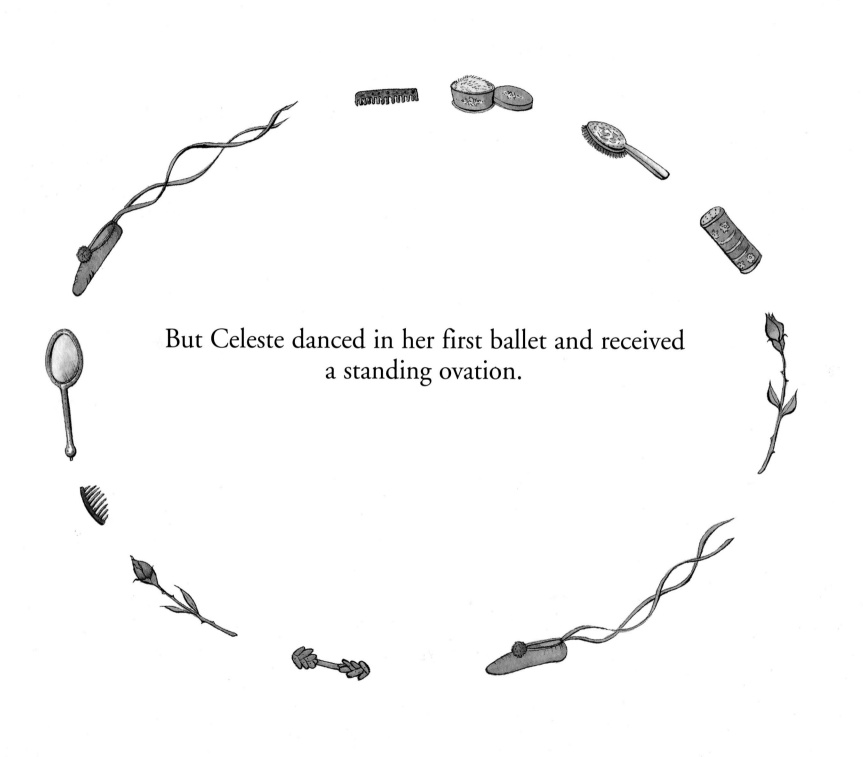

But Celeste danced in her first ballet and received
a standing ovation.

Five

 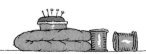

When Ernie was five
he was sure a monster
lived in his closet.

Celeste made a
snowman.

Rosie got a baby sister.

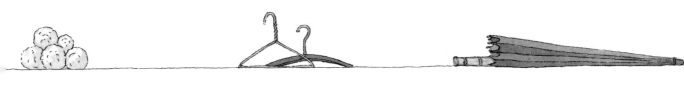

Nicky broke her arm.

Clive's mother sewed
his alligator suit.

And Tessa swam right
across the pool.

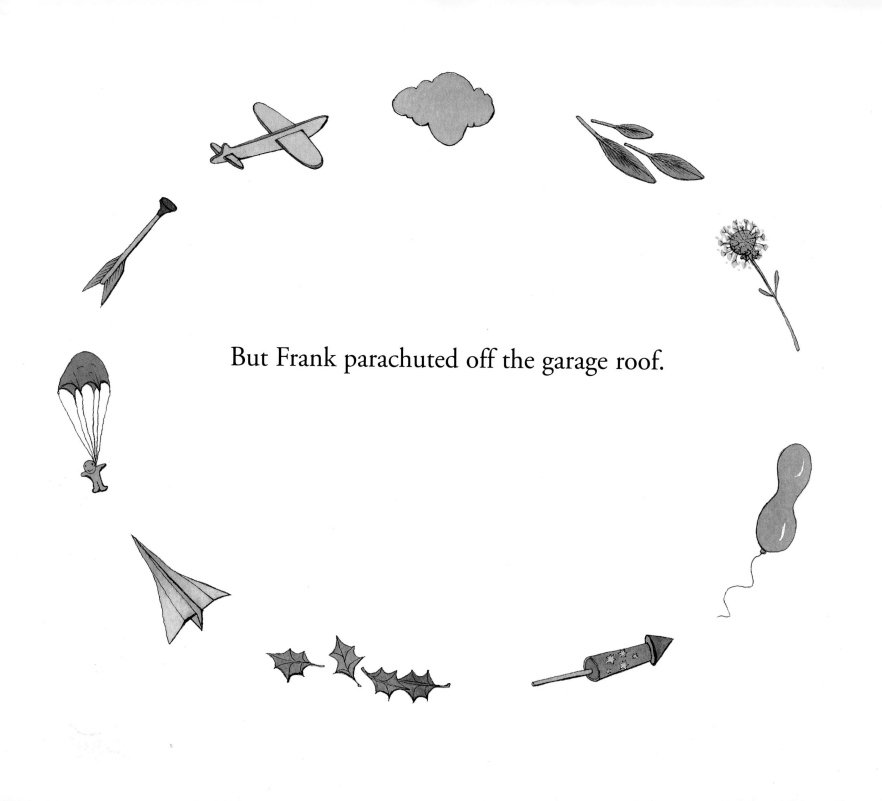

But Frank parachuted off the garage roof.

Six

When Nicky was six she did a somersault on the trampoline.

Frank kidnapped his Grandmother's cat.

Ernie's lizard had babies.

Clive made a
crocodile-shaped
birthday cake.

Tessa ran away from
home.

And Celeste wore her
pajama pants to
school.

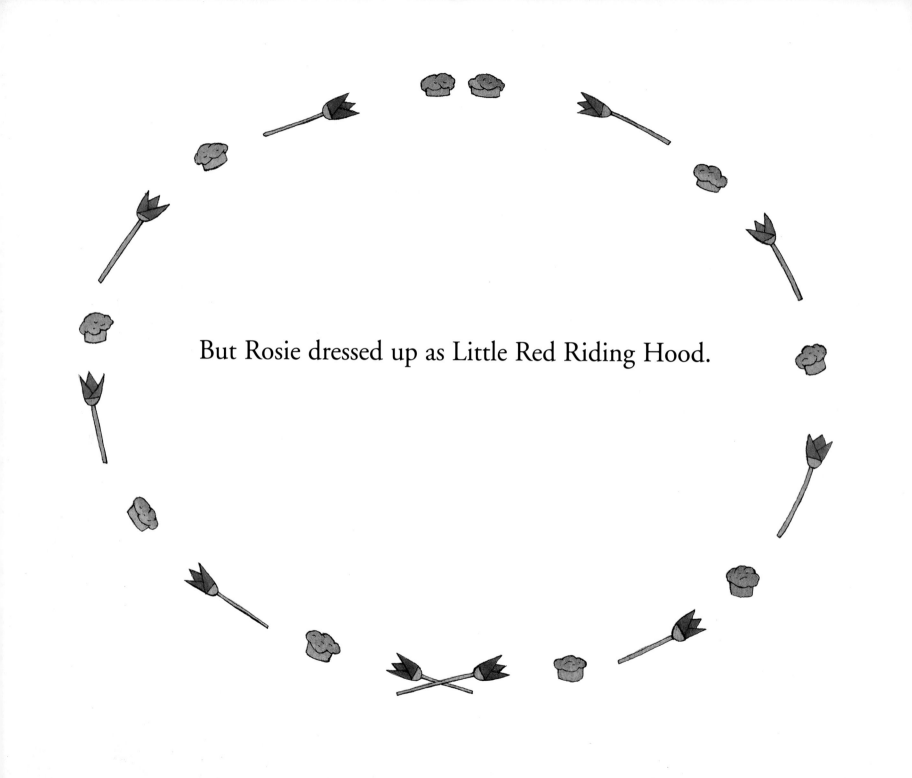

But Rosie dressed up as Little Red Riding Hood.

 # Seven

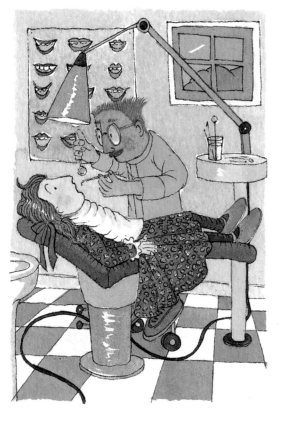

When Celeste was seven
she had her first filling.

Nicky flew off the swing.

Rosie climbed Uluru.

Frank built a spaceship.   And Tessa gave Clive his first kiss.

But Ernie made a midnight friend.

Clive has	1 alligator suit	2 goldfish	3 mixing bowls
Nicky has	1 rag doll	2 bouncing balls	3 hammers
Tessa has	1 calico cat	2 bunny slippers	3 wooden spoons
Celeste has	1 rooster	2 tutus	3 birthday balloons
Frank has	1 dog	2 rockets	3 bags of candy
Rosie has	1 cowgirl hat	2 riding boots	3 show ribbons
Ernie has	1 pacifier	2 saucepan lids	3 dinosaurs

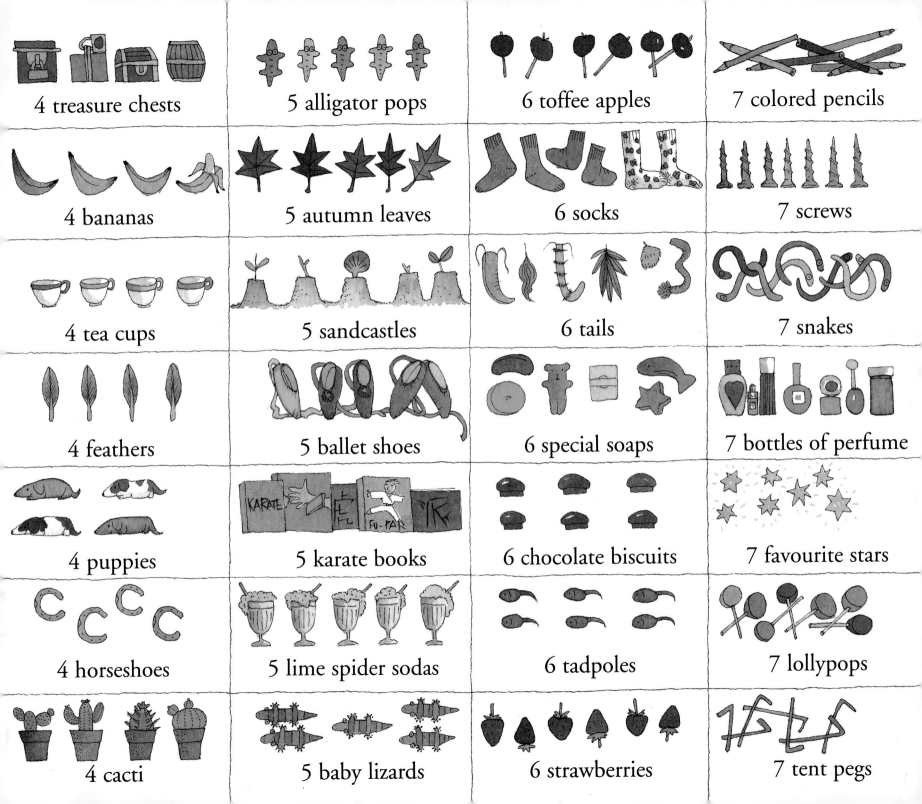

4 treasure chests	5 alligator pops	6 toffee apples	7 colored pencils
4 bananas	5 autumn leaves	6 socks	7 screws
4 tea cups	5 sandcastles	6 tails	7 snakes
4 feathers	5 ballet shoes	6 special soaps	7 bottles of perfume
4 puppies	5 karate books	6 chocolate biscuits	7 favourite stars
4 horseshoes	5 lime spider sodas	6 tadpoles	7 lollypops
4 cacti	5 baby lizards	6 strawberries	7 tent pegs

For Helen and Woofa

Walter Lorraine (wl) Books

Library of Congress Cataloging-in-Publication Data

Lester, Alison.
    When Frank was four / Alison Lester.
         p.   cm.
    Summary: Describes the new accomplishments and
experiences of seven children from the time they are one-year-
olds until they reach the age of seven.
    ISBN 0-395-74275-7 (hc)
    [1. Growth--Fiction. 2. Counting.]   I. Title.
PZ7.L56284Wh   1996   95-38276
[E]--dc20   CIP
                                                    AC

Printed in Hong Kong
Produced by Mandarin Offset
10 9 8 7 6 5 4 3 2 1

10/96